IT TAKES TEAMWORK!

Adapted by Margaret Green

"That's the sound of me still waking up," Ty explained. "Give me a minute, will you?"

So Revvit began counting. Ty laughed and stopped him. They raced over to the site of the new garage the Dinotrux and Reptools were building together. Ty loved the new plans the Reptools had drawn up and couldn't wait to get started.

"Come on, everyone, let's trux it up!" he said.

IT TAKES TEAMWORK!

Adapted by Margaret Green

Little, Brown and Company

Hachette Book Group
1290 Avenue of the Americas, New York, NY 10104
Visit us at lb-kids.com

LB kids is an imprint of Little, Brown and Company.
The LB kids name and logo are trademarks of Hachette Book Group, Inc.

The publisher is not responsible for websites (or their content) that are not owned by the publisher.

First Edition: April 2016

Library of Congress Control Number: 2015946001

ISBN: 978-0-316-26077-0

10 9 8 7 6 5 4 3 2 1

CW

Printed in the United States of America

Ty the Tyrannosaurus Trux stretched and yawned as he lumbered out of his cave one morning. As soon as his friend Revvit the Reptool saw that Ty was awake, he hurried over.

"Good. You are up," Revvit said. "Waldo, Ace, Click-Clack, and I have been going over the plans for the garage, and we have a couple small modifications to discuss—"

"Revvit, do you hear that?" Ty interrupted. Revvit stopped talking.

"That's the sound of me still waking up," Ty explained. "Give me a minute, will you?"

So Revvit began counting. Ty laughed and stopped him. They raced over to the site of the new garage the Dinotrux and Reptools were building together. Ty loved the new plans the Reptools had drawn up and couldn't wait to get started.

"Come on, everyone, let's trux it up!" he said.

"Before we begin building the garage, we should make sure everyone is in tip-top condition," Revvit suggested. He and the other Reptools made a few repairs on the Dinotrux.

The Dinotrux and Reptools were so busy working, they didn't notice that someone was spying on them. D-Structs, a Tyrannosaurus Trux who wanted the crater to himself, watched the Reptools as they fixed the Dinotrux's broken parts. Then he looked at his own damaged tail and growled.

Then D-Structs noticed a Scraptool named Skrap-It and had an idea. He rolled toward Skrap-It and loomed over him menacingly.

"My tail is broken," he said, swinging it around and slamming it down in front of Skrap-It. "Fix it."

"But I'm a Scraptool, not a Reptool," Skrap-It explained. "Reptools fix stuff. We take stuff apart."

"So do it backward," D-Structs said.

"What's in it for me?" asked Skrap-It.

"If you fix me, I'll give you a T-Trux to scrap," promised D-Structs.

Meanwhile, the Dinotrux were having a little trouble staying organized as they worked on building the garage. Dozer accidentally filled in the holes Ty made for the foundation, and Ton-Ton tossed a load of rocks onto Skya's logs, splintering them.

"Are they working off the same plans we are?" asked Ace.

"Give them time," said Revvit. "They are new at working together."

In the midst of all the chaos, Skrap-It snuck onto the construction site and stole a tail bolt that he needed to fix D-Structs's tail.

Skrap-It hid behind a rock with the tail bolt and watched as Ty called all the Dinotrux together. "This isn't working at all," Ty said.

"What are you talking about?" said Ton-Ton. "We've got one wall up already!" As he spoke, the wall came tumbling down. The Dinotrux immediately began fighting and blaming one another for messing things up.

"Guys!" Ty shouted. "We really have to find a way to work together."

Skrap-It hurried back to D-Structs and began installing the new tail bolt. As he worked, he told the T-Trux how the Dinotrux were fighting more than building.

D-Structs liked hearing that. "With a little help, their arguing will end their building and split their group apart for good," he said.

Back at the garage site, things kept going wrong—even though the Dinotrux were trying to work together.

"Ton-Ton!" Skya said angrily. "What did you do to my trees?" Her logs had once again been smashed by boulders.

"It wasn't me," Ton-Ton insisted.

Then Dozer found a bunch of trees sticking out of his rock mound and accused Skya of putting them there.

"It wasn't me!" she said. "It was probably Ton-Ton!"

What the Dinotrux didn't know was that D-Structs had flung the boulders and destroyed Dozer's mound.

"It's working, it's working!" Skrap-It said excitedly. "They're all fighting."

"And soon they'll all be leaving," said D-Structs. "They just need one more push." He flung a giant rock at the wall Ty had built, smashing it to the ground.

As the Reptools watched, the fighting got worse. Soon the Dinotrux were ramming into one another.

"What's the matter with all of you?" Ty shouted.

"Nothing that getting away from here can't fix!" declared Dozer, trucking off.

"Wherever he's going, I'm going the other way," said Ton-Ton. All three Dinotrux went off in different directions.

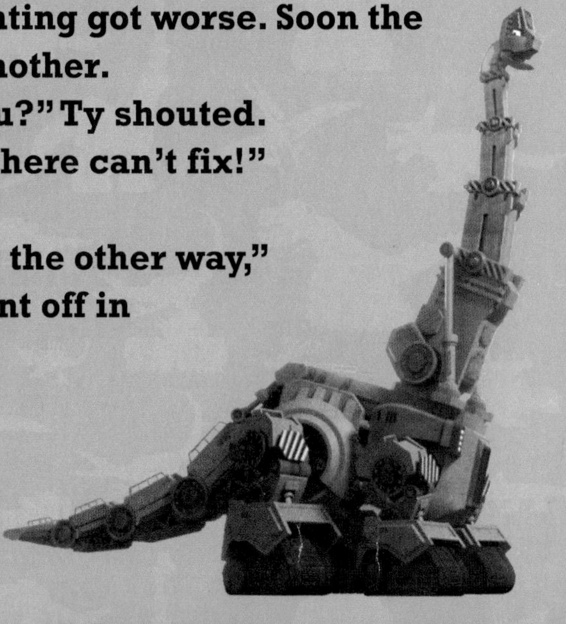

Now that Ty was alone, D-Structs was ready to face him. "Where are your friends, Ty?" He chuckled. "I hope you haven't been fighting."

Ty gasped. "You did this!"

D-Structs smiled. "You did it yourselves. You just needed a little push." With that, he swung his tail at Ty, sending him flying off the cliff.

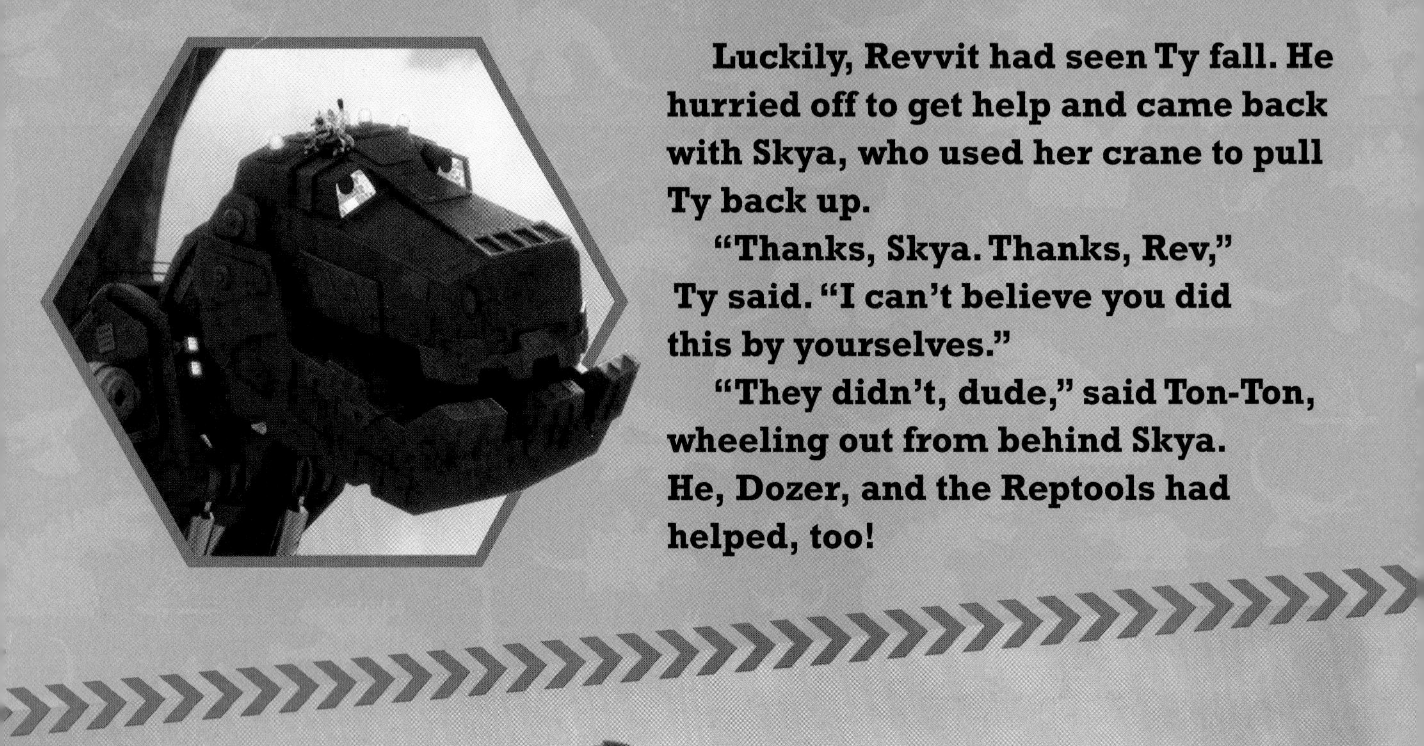

Luckily, Revvit had seen Ty fall. He hurried off to get help and came back with Skya, who used her crane to pull Ty back up.

"Thanks, Skya. Thanks, Rev," Ty said. "I can't believe you did this by yourselves."

"They didn't, dude," said Ton-Ton, wheeling out from behind Skya. He, Dozer, and the Reptools had helped, too!

"Revvit told us what happened," Dozer explained. "Now let's show D-Structs what happens when you mess with us!"

"Yeah!" cheered Ton-Ton and Skya.

"No!" said Ty. "If we fight him, he'll just come back later, stronger."

"We need to prove to him that we cannot be broken up so easily," Revvit said.

"And I know just how to do it," said Ty. "We're going to finish what we started. Together."

The Dinotrux got to work finishing their garage.

Dozer and Ty dug a foundation hole.

Then Ton-Ton tossed Ty a rock to fill it with.

Dozer dozed up a mound of boulders for Skya.

And the Reptools used their scoring bits to shape the garage walls.

Soon the garage was almost finished. But Revvit realized they'd forgotten something! "We made the garage so large, there are no trees big enough for a roof."

"I think I know something else that could work," Ty said, pointing up at the giant flat rock that towered over the garage.

Working together, the Dinotrux and Reptools carefully pulled the rock down until it fell right on top of the walls of the garage. It was finally finished!

D-Structs and Skrap-It approached the garage.

"They finished it?" Skrap-It said with a twitch.

"I don't understand," said D-Structs.

"That's exactly your problem, D-Structs," said Ty, surrounded by all his Dinotrux friends. "You'll never understand."

D-Structs knew he couldn't win against all the Dinotrux. He backed away into the forest.

"Uh, dudes?" said Ton-Ton. "I don't know about you, but I'm kind of itching to try this garage out."

"You're going to have to beat me to it," said Ty. The Dinotrux and the Reptools took off toward the garage they had built—together.